ISIMEME'S STORIES

Nnenna and her udara tree
Why the bat flies at night
Onye and Tunde

Isimeme's Stories
©1993 Text by Isimeme Ibazebo
©1993 Illustrations by John Hurford

Distributed in the United States by
The Wright Group
19201 120th Avenue NE
Bothell, WA 98011-9512

First published in the United Kingdom in 1993 by
Spindlewood
70 Lynhurst Avenue
Barnstaple, Devon EX31 2HY

Printed by Paramount Printing Group, Hong Kong

10 9 8 7 6 5 4 3 2 1

ISBN: 0-907349-02-1

ISIMEME'S STORIES

Isimeme Ibazebo

Illustrated by John Hurford

Spindlewood

Nnenna and her udara tree

ONCE, not so very long ago, there was a young girl who lived with her father in a small village in Nsukka. Her name was Nnenna. She had lovely, shiny black hair and soft, smooth skin. Now Nnenna's mother had died a few months earlier, and her father was still feeling very unhappy. Nnenna tried her best to raise her father's spirits. She cooked all his favourite meals. She cleaned his treasured ornaments. She even polished his hoe every night, just as she had seen her mother do. But her father still looked unhappy.

One day, Nnenna's father came back from the farm looking very excited. He had a great big smile on his face. Nnenna was glad to see him in such good spirits. She picked up the fresh corn and yams he had brought back with him. After washing them, she went into the backyard to start the fire.
That night, as they sat by the fire roasting the corn, Nnenna's father told her why he was looking so happy.
"I met a very nice woman to-day," he began. "I've invited her round on Sunday. Her name is Mrs Ezelu and she lives by the edge of the farm. I think she just moved there."
Nnenna didn't say anything. She was glad her father was looking his old self again. After the moon rose, Nnenna's father went into the house. He whistled as he took off his work clothes. For the first time in weeks he slept soundly.

Mrs Ezelu and her children arrived early on Sunday morning. Nnenna had dusted and cleaned the house. It was sparkling. The meal they had prepared was delicious – garri with banga soup. After eating, Mrs Ezelu insisted on washing up all the plates.

"Both of you have done enough for one day," she said. "Go and rest your feet. I'll look after everything."

Nnenna did not need any convincing. She had been up early that day and cooking the meal had exhausted her. Nnenna took her mat into the yard and lay down for an afternoon nap.

The wedding ceremony followed soon after, and Mrs Ezelu and her children moved in. Nnenna was pleased because she could see that her father was very happy. And she thought Mrs Ezelu was a nice enough woman.

Once Mrs Ezelu had settled in, as Nnenna's stepmother her attitude towards Nnenna changed. She never let Nnenna rest, shouting and screaming at her.

"Don't just sit there, you horrible girl," she would say when Nnenna got back from school. "Come on, go and wash the children's clothes. And then wash the plates. And when you have finished that let me know. There is plenty of work to do around here, lazy girl."

Nnenna would hurry off to do the chores. She would scrub the floor, do the dishes, cook the meal. Then she would sweep the yard. She was always so tired when she finished she could barely eat any food. This went on for days and days. Nnenna grew very unhappy and lost a lot of weight. And although her father kept asking her what was wrong, she didn't want to tell him, for she didn't want to cause any trouble.

One day, Mrs Ezelu bought some fruit called udara from the market. She gave each of her children some of the fruit, but didn't give any to Nnenna.

"Go and clean the stove. Then sweep the yard again. Some dry leaves have fallen this afternoon. I'm not going to waste any udara on you." Nnenna went off to do as she was told.

She picked up the dried leaves in the back yard. Then she began to sweep the yard. She saw one of the udara seeds lying on the ground. Nnenna planted it next to the large palm tree, and as she covered it with soil, she sang very gently,

> "Udara grow
> grow, grow, grow.
> My father's wife
> bought udara in the market
> and ate it all up.
> Ate it all up without giving me any."

To Nnenna's surprise, the seed started sprouting before her very eyes. The more Nnenna sang, the more the seedling grew. But her stepmother called her in and she left the little tree.

The next day when Nnenna finished her chores, she rushed to the yard and, as soon as she sang gently to the tree, it began to grow again. Nnenna went back into the house later on, but she was still grinning. "What are you so happy about?" her stepmother asked. "Go and wash all the plates. That should wipe the grin off your face." But Nnenna kept smiling.

All through the next week, Nnenna spent as much time as she could with her tree. By the end of the week the fruits were ripe and ready to eat. Nnenna climbed happily up the tree and picked some of the fruits. Then she sat up there eating them.

For three weeks Nnenna kept her secret. Her stepmother never came out into the yard and the children always played out in front. She spent all her evenings singing in her tree, which grew bigger and bigger. But on the fourth week, Nnenna got back from school to see her stepmother high up the tree.

"That's my tree, Mama," Nnenna yelled. "I planted it from a seed you threw away."

"What rubbish. How can a tree grow so quickly?" her stepmother replied scornfully. "If you don't stop your lies I will give you a good beating."

"But I am not telling lies . . ."

"Just keep quiet," the stepmother cut in. And hissing, she began to climb even higher.

Nnenna began to sing her song and the udara tree began to grow taller and taller. Her stepmother began to scream, "Nnenna, do something! Why is the tree growing bigger?"

"Because of the song," Nnenna answered. "That's how it grew so big in the first place."

Nnenna continued singing.

Her stepmother was really frightened. "To think Nnenna has this kind of power, and I have been treating her so badly," she said to herself. She began to cry.

"Please stop singing. I promise I won't treat you badly again."

Nnenna felt sorry for her stepmother. She stopped singing and helped her climb down. They walked back into the house.

The stepmother was never unkind to Nnenna again. As for the udara tree, it never grew any larger, even though Nnenna sang and sang till her voice was hoarse. But Nnenna didn't really mind. At least she wasn't unhappy any more.

Why the bat flies at night

MANY, many years ago, a group of animals lived together on the edge of the Kalahari Desert.   They were all great friends with each other.   Cuckoo ate from the same bowl as Lion, and Vulture shared a hut with Squirrel.   The animals that could fly did not call themselves birds and those that walked around did not call themselves mammals. They were all just plain animals.

There was plenty of food for the animals.   Bunches of ripe bananas appeared on the trees every week, okra and melons sprouted wherever their seeds fell and the lakes and streams never dried up.   But there was one fruit that was in very short supply, the pawpaw.   The animals loved eating pawpaws more than any other fruit, but the only tree on the edge of the desert produced twelve pawpaws a year, barely enough to go round for them all.

One year the pawpaw tree bore no fruits at all.   Lion spent so much time dreaming about pawpaws that his mouth began to water.   Poor Owl flew round and round the tree looking for new fruits for so long he began to feel quite dizzy.   The animals did the best they could to help their tree bear fruit.   They watered and weeded and fed the tree until, at last, after many, many months a pawpaw appeared.

"Well," Lion said smugly, "after all my efforts, at last my pawpaw is coming."

"Your pawpaw?" Owl replied. "What do you mean your pawpaw? It's not just for you, you know."

"I've spent every single night under this tree. I've watched over it like a baby," said Lion.

"What about me?" Owl replied angrily. "My wings are about to drop off."

"Oh, rubbish!" said Lion. "We land animals did most of the work. We are bigger and stronger than you flying animals. Yes, we. . .er. . . yes, we mammals should get a larger share than you birds."

"What do you mean by mammals and birds?" said Owl. "So you have thought up new names for us all, eh?"

For days Owl and Lion sat under the pawpaw tree arguing about which side deserved the bigger share, and as they argued the pawpaw grew bigger and riper and juicier. Finally, they reached a decision. The mammals and birds would have a fight, and the winning side would keep the whole pawpaw.

That evening Lion called a meeting between all the mammals and told them what had happened.

"This is what we are going to do," Lion began. "We will attack the birds while they are asleep tonight. They won't be ready for us. I am sure it will be all over in minutes."

Late that night, before the moon had fully risen, the mammals crept over to the birds and began their attack. All seemed to be going well, and Lion's tummy began to rumble in anticipation.

Suddenly, Bat, who had joined the birds in the first place, began to speak in a loud voice, "Wait, oh wait! I'm not really a bird, you know. I'm warm-blooded.   I have hair like the rest of the mammals.   I don't lay eggs.   I'm on the wrong side!" Bat did not want to miss out on having some of the pawpaw.

As he spoke, Bat joined the mammals, but the birds fought back bravely.   After a while the mammals retreated and went to lie down beside the lake.

The birds gathered round Owl to plan what they were going to do. "We will fly off and attack them right away," Owl said, in a hushed voice.   "They will be so tired they won't be able to fight back.   I will fight Lion.   You, Ostrich, will attack Hyena . . ." With this they flew onto the mammals, pecking with their beaks and scratching with their claws.   The attack was going very, very well and then Bat began to speak.

"Haba!" he yelled, "I'm not really a mammal, you know.   I'm a bird. After all, I have wings like a bird.   I can fly.   Mmm, I'm on the wrong side again."   And greedy Bat went over to join the birds.

The fight between the birds and mammals went on for days. Whenever the mammals appeared to be winning, Bat would say he was a mammal and if the birds appeared to be winning, Bat would say he was a bird.

But the animals grew very tired and after a week Lion and Owl decided to call a truce.

"We will share the pawpaw equally between the mammals and the birds," said Lion.

Soon all the animals were enjoying the delicious fruit, except for poor greedy Bat, who hovered between Lion and Owl. He didn't know who to go to.

"You are not really a bird, are you?" said Owl, as Bat stretched out his claws for a piece of the pawpaw.

"Neither are you a mammal," said Lion. "We must punish him. From now on you do not belong to my family of mammals."

"Yes, and from now on we birds don't want anything to do with you either," Owl added.

All the animals began to laugh at Bat. Poor Bat was so ashamed he rushed off to hide in a coconut tree. He swore he would never let any of the animals see him again. But he still had to eat, so each night he left his hiding place to search for food. And that is why today Bat only comes out at night.

Onye and Tunde

ONCE upon a time, in the village of Opobo, there lived a rich man called Tunde and a poor man called Onye.   Tunde and Onye had grown up together.   They were still good friends.   Tunde owned the biggest farm in the village and lived in the grandest house.   Onye spent his days working on Tunde's farm, tilling the soil and planting seeds.   In the evenings, he would pick up his hoe and go over to his friend's house.   Tunde always had a big meal cooking for his rich friends and he never minded giving Onye a little from his pot.

One year, a great famine broke out in the village.   The grass got browner and browner and the rivers dried up.   All the fish in the rivers had to be scooped up and, since there were no fridges in those days, the villagers had to eat all the fish before they became rotten.   The crops on Tunde's farm all withered away and died.   Tunde had to ask his workers to go home until the rains began again.   Onye, of course, was one of them.   He went home dejectedly, wondering where his next meal would come from.   He knew Tunde wouldn't want to give him any free meals from his pot.   Besides, Tunde had stopped having his big parties since the famine began.   As Onye walked towards his house, a little boy saw how unhappy he was and offered him a few husks of corn.
"Oh, thank you very much," Onye cried out.   "May God bless you, my son."

Onye rushed home to cook his corn, but he had no chicken to make a good pot of soup and he didn't even have any salt or pepper to season the meal.   Onye cooked his corn and began to eat it.   It tasted horrible.

"I know what I'll do," he cried out loudly.   "I'm sure Tunde will be cooking something for himself.   I'll take my corn and go off to his house.   His soup will surely smell very nice.   I can sit outside his kitchen window and eat my corn.   With the sweet smell from his cooking, I can imagine I'm eating a tasty meal."

And off Onye went towards his friend's house.   Just as he expected, Tunde was cooking a delicious pot of soup.   The smells coming out from his kitchen were marvellous.   Onye sat under the kitchen window and, closing his eyes, began to eat the corn.   Once he had finished his meal he hurried back home.

The next day Onye bumped into his friend in the village square.

"Oh, what a lovely pot of soup you were cooking last night. I sat beneath your window and inhaled the sweet smells. My corn tasted much better, thanks to you."

"So, that is why my food tasted so bad last night," yelled Tunde. "You stole the sweet smell and taste from my food. You must pay me back!"

"I didn't steal anything from you," Onye began in a hurt voice. "All I did was . . ."

"You must pay me back," Tunde cut in angrily. "I demand a newly-born goat. If you don't bring it round to my house by tomorrow evening, I will seize everything you own."

"Come now, Tunde. What is the big problem? Ah, ah, it's me now, your friend, remember?"

But Tunde would not listen. He had become very selfish and greedy since the famine started. He had hidden food from his servants and cut their wages. He had even taken all the jewellery back from his wife, in case they needed to sell it, he said. His greed had got the better of him. He was looking forward to getting a free goat.

Onye walked around the village, looking even more miserable than ever.

"What am I going to do?" he thought to himself. "I have no money to buy a goat even if I wanted to."

He walked around the village square for hours. Finally, Onye decided to take the matter before the wise elder of the village, a man called Okosun.

Okusun was the oldest man in the village.   Nobody knew exactly how old he was.   Some said he was born before the great rivers by the village were formed.   Others said he had been placed in the village by the God of Thunder himself.   Okusun looked old and frail, but he was the strongest man around for miles.

As Onye approached his hut, Okusun called out to him in a kind voice, "Come in, my son.   Tell me what is troubling you."
When Onye told him what had happened between him and Tunde, Okusun was very angry.
"Don't worry," he said.   "Leave everything to me.   Take this goat and meet me in the village square tomorrow evening.   Tell Tunde to be there as well.   I, as the eldest in the village, will judge this case."
Onye was relieved.   At last, he could go home and have a proper night's sleep.   No more worries.
Onye popped into Tunde's house on his way home, with the goat at his side.
"Oh, I see you have my goat.   Good, good," Tunde said in a happy voice.   "Yes, I'll see you tomorrow at the square.   I wouldn't miss collecting my goat for anything."

The next evening, all the villagers gathered around the square to see what would happen. Okusun sat in the middle on a high chair. Onye, looking harassed and unhappy, arrived soon after Tunde, dragging the goat behind him.

"Well, my sons," Okusun began, "I have heard your story. Will you let me pass judgement on the case?"

"Yes," they both replied. "You be the judge."

"Very well, Tunde," the old man said. "Get ready for your payment. Onye, I want you to hit the goat. Go on, hit it."

Onye did as he was told.

"Now, Tunde, I want you to take the goat's bleating as payment for the taste and smell of your food. Since Onye did not eat any of your food, you can't eat his goat."

All the villagers smiled. For Okosun was quite right. The goat's bleating was payment enough.

Of course, Tunde was furious, but there was nothing he could do. An elder always had the last say.

Everyone went home smiling. Everyone except Tunde. Okosun continued to give wise and fair judgements, and Onye continued to live in his house. As for Tunde, no one in the village spoke to him ever again.